D1739250

1

Four to Go

Jay Crowley

ALSO BY JAY CROWLEY

Natalie Adventures © Youth

Cabin in the Meadow © Novella

A Ship in the Desert©

Opal©

Laura ©

My Selections of Short Stories ©

A Gift from Nate-Story of a Double Lung Transplant © Non-Fiction

Not Worthy-Story of Revenge © Novella

Maggie ©

Drum of Hope ©

Lahontan City©

Topaz©

Treasurer Stuck in Time ©

ANTHOLOGIES

Other Realms I & II

Heard it on the Radio

13 Bites III & IV

Free for All

From Outer Space MK II & III

559 Ways to Die

The Collapse Directive

Tales of Southwest

Relationship Add-Vice

Christmas Lites VII, VIII, and IX

Around the World

AWARDS

Who's Who of Emerging Authors 2020, 2021?

National Novel Writing Month for 2017, 2018, 2019, 2020, and 2021

I, Jay Crowley, Writer

The research for the story and places came from Wikipedia, friends, and my memories.

Dedication

As always, I dedicate my books to my readers. Without you, I wouldn't be writing.

I want to thank the alpha readers, Colin Canter, Bob Pifer, Cindy Gower, and Carla Douglas. Special thanks to the beta readers, Josie Leeds, Ann Mori, and my hubby Tom Crowley. My writing requires their eyes to find the spelling and punctuation errors and see how the story flows. We couldn't do it without them.

After my last story, "Treasure Stuck in Time," I thought of retiring Maggie, Nan, and the Wild Stitchers as I introduced a new character, Nick. However, the Wild Stitchers are again involved in this story due to Maggie's friendship with one of the characters. You will marvel at this story of survivorship.

Always appreciate hearing from you about any of my stories. Thanks for your support over all these years.

Sincerely,

Jay Crowley

Chapter One

Eight-year-old Chad was chasing his six-year-old sister Bunny through the house, and they both were screaming like kids do.

"Enough!" Shouted their mother, Winona. *Darn, I don't care if it's only eleven,* "I'm sending you to the schoolyard to play. You guys can burn off some of that energy."

She was nursing three-month-old Lenora in a nursing sling as she got Bunny warmly dressed in a hat and mittens. Chad was able to dress himself. They both put their boots on.

"You can stay playing in the schoolyard for an hour." Winona had taught both children how to tell time on the old-school analog clock.

Hopefully, they would be ready for a nap when they came home at the end of the hour. Winona laid the baby down in her crib as the kids ran out the door.

Thank goodness her four-year-old, Billy, was still asleep. Her husband, Chad Sr., drove a snow plow for the Nevada Department of Transportation. They expect a big snowstorm this afternoon, so he would probably be working overtime.

After everybody left and the baby was down, Winona finally had peace and quiet for a few minutes. *Now to do my chores. At least the laundry is quiet, as she laughed to herself.*

Chapter Two

The kids ran to the schoolyard about one block away. Kids living in Schurz didn't have to worry about crime, or so they thought.

Chad ran to the monkey bars, removing his gloves to shove in his back pocket. He joined some of his friends. Bunny started swinging with a couple of her girlfriends. Apparently, a lot of kids were bored.

The girls swung for a while before they spotted the hopscotch game under some snow. Using their feet to clear it off, they started playing. Bunny removed her boots to play as they were cumbersome.

The first is to start, rest, then jump, two for the money, rest, then jump, three for the show, rest, then jump, four to go, and the last jump to end the game. The game's premise is to do it fast—the fastest wins.

After about three games, Bunny's mom's sister Clara drove up and waved for her to come to her car. Bunny looked at the clock. It wasn't time for her to go home yet. Chad saw his Aunt Clara drive up and started heading over to her. She waved him back. *Wonder what is up?* But then, one of his friends called him, so he returned to the monkey bars.

Bunny apprehensively approached the car. She thought. *Why is she here?*

"Get in. I haven't seen you in a while. I'll take you for an ice cream cone to catch up," explained Clara.

Bunny didn't hesitate at the mention of ice cream and got in the car. As they drove off, she put her head out the window and stuck her tongue out at her brother.

"How have you been? It's been a while since I've seen you," mentioned Clara.

Bunny thought. *My family says we don't see you because of your lazy, drunken husband.* But Bunny didn't say anything about that.

Bunny did say, "You drove past the store."

"Yes, I did, as I have to take something to a friend, it's just a little way down the road," explained her aunt. Bunny thought. *I'll be late getting home, and I forgot my boots.*

They turned down Hwy 95 toward Hawthorne. After a couple of miles, Clara took a dirt road which seemed to take forever. Finally, they pulled up to an old shack in the mountains.

"We won't be long. Come on in with me to meet them," smiled Clara.

Bunny wasn't pleased about going in. She was bashful about meeting new people, especially if they're friends of Clara. Bunny stayed behind Clara as they walked up and knocked on the door. It opened quickly, and there stood a tall thin man with wild-looking shoulder-length brown hair and long brown whiskers down his belly. "Come on in. Glad you made it," he said, smiling.

Clara grabbed Bunny and pushed her in as she followed. Bunny looked around the two-room shack. She saw some other children hiding in another room, peeking out. *Who are these people,* Bunny thought?

"I brought her just like I said I would. Now I want my money," whined Clara. Bunny's eyes grew wide. *What in the heck is happening?* She stared at her aunt.

"Everything is going to be okay," stated Clara. Bunny shook her head and started to leave. Clara grabbed her and held her tight.

"What kind of person are you to sell your niece to me?" asked the man.

"Someone who needs the ten thousand you promised me. Her mother has three other children and can have more, so she won't miss this one," explained Clara coldly.

The man quietly said to Bunny, "Go join the other children." Bunny looked in the direction he pointed. Clara let go of her. She hesitated and then promptly ran over to the kids. They all huddled together. *What was going on?* Thought Bunny.

Clara whined again, "Give me my money so I can get home before the storm hits."

"You're a very cold, heartless person," said the man.

"I don't care what you think of me. Just give me my money."

He reached into the bag behind him like he was reaching for money; instead, he pulled out a pistol and shot Clara twice in the chest. The children screamed.

The man turned toward the kids and shouted, "Quiet! Children, take your pillow and blanket and get into the truck outside."

Bunny just stood there frozen. "Do you have a problem, girl?" he shouted.

"'Yes. I don't have a pillow and blanket," she stammered.

"Aaron, show the girl where her stuff is." Aaron ran into the room and grabbed the blanket and pillow off the floor, giving them to Bunny. Then all four kids ran out the door to the four-door primer gray Dodge Dakota truck.

The boys sat in front and the girls in the back. Nobody said a word. They were too scared. Was the man going to kill them?

After Aaron got in and looked around the truck, he said, "Wow, I know how to drive this truck, and the keys are in the ignition. We are getting the heck out of here before he kills us."

He quickly fired it up and started driving down the road.

The man didn't hear the truck start over the roar of the fire he had initiated but caught the truck out of the corner of his eye as it drove down the road. *Darn, kids!*

He quickly jumped in Clara's car, but no keys! He had burned them up with her. *Well, that didn't work out as I had planned*, as he hit the steering wheel several times in frustration.

Getting out of the car, kicking the dirt, and cussing to himself, he started walking down the road as a light snow began. It took him a good hour to make it to the main road. The snow was starting to stick now.

He was wet and cold, and his jacket hadn't helped much, when he flagged down a big rig headed toward Yerington. He was thankful the truck's cab was warm when he hopped in.

Tomorrow was another day. However, he had to find those kids. His plan wouldn't work without them. Plus, they knew too much to be running loose. *Where did they go? Did they go to the Sheriff's office in Hawthorne?*

Thank goodness the driver didn't ask why he was out hitchhiking in a snowstorm. The man just sat there, not talking to the driver but fuming about his stupidity to let the kids escape.

Chapter Three

When Chad got home with no little sister, but he had her boots, he told his mom that Aunt Clara had taken her and thought they had gone to the store. Winona thought *Clara probably took her shopping, but she had never done that before, but she is my unpredictable sister.* She didn't worry. *However, that isn't like Clara. She must want something.*

After several hours, and with the snow sticking now, Winona started to worry about her sister and daughter.

Winona called the store. "No, we hadn't seen either one of them."

She then called Clara's home, and her drunken husband answered. "Sorry, Hon, I haven't seen her all day, but she better get home before the snow gets heavier as she has the beer... ha-ha."

Now, Winona was beside herself. Where could they be? She tried her sister's cell, but it went to voice mail. She called Chad Sr, but as usual, he couldn't hear the phone over the sound of the plow, so she left a message, "Call home."

The snow was coming down in big flakes, covering the ground. *Where could they be?* Winona wondered if Clara had an accident. A thousand things went through her mind. *Should I call Tribal?* After fifteen minutes of pacing, she called. It was after four in the afternoon.

Winona told the Tribal office that her daughter and sister were overdue getting home. She gave them the names. What she then heard wasn't good news.

They had a report from the Mineral County Sheriff's Office of a fire on a back road in the mountains outside of Hawthorne. A car parked at the fire scene was registered to Hank and Clara Pamahas, address in Schurz.

No one was around, but they found a body in the burned building. It's not been identified, but it's an adult woman. Winona got off the phone shaking. *Where was her Bunny? And why would Clara be down there?*

Chad was being the big brother and playing with Billy. He didn't know what was happening, but he knew his mom needed his help. Lenora started crying. She wanted to eat. Winona changed her and began nursing her. The phone rang, and Winona jumped up to answer. Thank goodness for the nursing sling, or she would have dropped the baby. *Calm down, lady. You're a mess.*

"Hello."

"Hi, hon. What is going on?" asked Chad Sr.

Between the sobs, "I can't find Bunny. Clara picked her up at the schoolyard," sobbing as she told him what had happened.

"I'll try to get off work and be home as soon as possible. This is going to be one heck of a storm, and we are short drivers," stated Chad.

"That would be awesome if you could come home. I'm beside myself. I hope you can get off," sobbed Winona. She sat back on the couch to feed the baby until Lenora fell asleep. She still had to fix something for Chad and Billy to eat.

She began cooking hotdogs and chili beans, which the kids loved, between the sobs. *I have children to take care of. Snap out of it. Everything will be okay. There's a logical explanation.*

Chapter Four

Aaron wasn't sure why he drove twenty-four miles south on Hwy 95 to Luning, then turned onto Hwy 361. The road goes to Gabbs and then ends around Middlegate. Aaron knew about this area. He often drove his drunken dad on this road to Middlegate for one last drink before getting home in Fallon. His dad liked to drink in Hawthorne as no one knew him there. Aaron reasoned *he wasn't thinking and was headed home in his mind.*

Aaron knew now he couldn't make it to Fallon or back to Hawthorne, not with all the snow coming down. However, he did remember a line shack where they could hide until the weather cleared. His dad liked to sleep off a good drunk there. The shack was located about two miles off the highway among the pinion pine and not visible from the main road. Due to its isolation, it was a great place to hide.

The snow was covering the ground as they arrived at the shack. Aaron parked the truck in the barn. The biggest thing they would have to worry about was warmth and food. He said, "We must gather the firewood from the porch. Hopefully, there might be some food in the shack, but doubt it."

Bunny said, "Well, if this is any help, three big bags of food are back here."

"Wahoo!" said Aaron. He came around to see and help pack them into the shack. They also carried their blankets and pillow from the truck.

The shack was one room with two windows, so there was plenty of daytime light. It was a little dusty but livable. It had a sink and a table-type counter but no water. A bed made of wood, with a thin mattress and pillow. They quickly brought in firewood. Also, Bunny found some kindling, at least enough for a few days, and newspapers by the bed, which would help to build a fire.

They laid out the large bags of food on the counter. There were three types of cereal, two boxes of mush, apple juice, four loaves of bread, and a large jar of peanut butter, canned goods, many with pop-top lids, large grape jelly, and four boxes of cookies.

"Wow. The man was prepared to feed us," explained the other girl.

Looking around the shelves, the kids found two cans of beans dated a few years back, a couple of good cans of peaches, and a bottle of whisky. They did this all without talking much.

The girl laughed as she looked at the cans, "Some of these cans won't do much good without a can opener or a metal spoon. You can open a can with a spoon. Did you know that? I'll keep looking."

She took over handling the food and placing it on the shelves.

Big snowflakes were coming down now, but the shack seemed able to keep them dry. It had one small gap in a wall, probably caused by an animal trying to get in. Aaron stuffed the old pillow from the bed in the hole. It helped. But tomorrow, they would pile snow to block any cold air or any animals from coming in.

They huddled in a circle around the fire, wrapped in blankets, eating peanut butter and jelly sandwiches that the girl had made. It didn't take long for the shack to get warm. The only light was from the windows, and it was getting dark outside.

Aaron said, "If you need to go to the bathroom, there is an outhouse by the back corner of the shack."

The girls went, "Uwe." Everyone laughed.

"Well, it is time to meet everyone," stated Aaron, with black curly hair, "we know each other," pointing to the girl and another boy. "But Bunny hadn't met us. I'm Aaron from Fallon. I'm ten, and I know I'm tall for my age, as I'm five feet, two inches. I've four older brothers over six feet tall and two older sisters. As the youngest in the family, my dad sold me to the man who then shot him. I was the first kid he purchased."

Everyone went whoa.

"Yeah, he locked us in the bedroom every time he went to get a new kid, except you, Bunny. There were three beds for us and a blanket and pillow on the floor," stated Aaron.

Rosa and Randy shook their head in agreement.

Rosa had beautiful brown eyes and dark brown hair. "Rosa is my name. I'm seven, almost eight. I come from Yerington. I've three older brothers. One of my brothers, who was into drugs, sold me to the man. He got killed too. I was the third kid he kidnaped."

Everyone said, "I'm sorry for your brother."

"I'm not. He sold me to a man who kills people," snapped Rosa. Everybody shook their head in agreement.

"Next. My name is Randy," a redhead with green eyes. "I come from Reno." Looking at Aaron, "I'm over four feet tall. I'll be seven in three weeks. I've three older sisters. No one sold me. He kidnapped me after Aaron's kidnapping from a local playground in Reno in the daytime! The sad part is no one tried to stop him, even with me screaming."

Everyone understood. They had seen that people never look up from their phones or don't want to get involved.

Bunny has dark hair, dark eyes, and an olive complexion. "My name is Bunny. I'm from Schurz. I'm six and going to be seven in June. I've got an older brother, a younger brother, and a baby sister. You know the rest about me." Bunny further added with a sly look, "Four to go."

"What do you mean by that?" questioned Rosa.

"It's a hopscotch game that fits us. We're four on the go..." laughed Bunny.

Everyone laughed.

Randy asked Aaron, "How did you know about this shack?"

Aaron responded, "As I said earlier, I drove my drunken dad on this road many times. He would stay here to sober up a bit before going home. I want to change the subject. The man once said he would make us rich... whatever that means. Did anyone hear him say it?"

Randy and Rosa shook their head yes. "But he never explained what he meant," said Randy.

"Yeah, he never tried to molest us and fed us well," explained Rosa.

Then Aaron asked what everyone was thinking, "I wonder why the man wanted us, four children from different towns and backgrounds?" No one knew the answer. No one knew the man. In fact, they said they had never seen him before, except Rosa, who thought maybe she had but wasn't sure.

Finally, they huddled together to stay warm during the night, as they knew the fire would go out before morning. Aaron thought he would wake up and feed the fire later but wasn't sure he would wake up in time. Tomorrow would be another day. At least now, they were safe, warm, and tummies full.

Chapter Five

The snow had been falling for several days. Maggie was sitting at her kitchen table drinking her coffee, watching it come down. "Well, I guess this time, the weather people were right. We must have close to a foot."

Pete was still not feeling well and was pretty much on oxygen 24/7, as he said from the couch, "Yep." All he does anymore is watch TV and play on his phone. He misses working with the 4H kids.

Maggie had her computer on the kitchen table, researching for a Nevada magazine article that was due in a couple of weeks. She was writing about Gabbs, Berlin State Park, and Ione. The phone rang, but she didn't recognize the number. *Probably scammers, they call all the time. The do-not-call thing doesn't work.*

She answered gruffly, "Hello."

"Oh, Maggie, I'm so glad you are home. I need to tell you what is going on, as I need your help," said the stressed voice on the other end of the line between sobs.

"May I ask who this is?" asked Maggie.

"Sorry, this is Win...Winona from Schurz. Darn, I'm so upset. I don't know who I am."

"I'm sorry, Winona, I didn't recognize your voice. It's been a while since I've talked to you."

"I know. Funny how time flies. I now have another child, making it four kids," Winona cried. "I need your help," again between sobs.

"What is going on? Hopefully, it's not that bad, and maybe we can fix the problem."

"My second child Bunny, you remember her? She's now six, almost seven. Several days ago, she disappeared." Winona proceeded to tell Maggie what had happened.

"Your sister took her? Clara? Yes, I do remember her and her interesting husband," laughed Maggie. "She took Bunny, and she has disappeared too?"

"Yes. The Mineral County Sheriff's Office found her car by a burned shack in the mountain outside of Hawthorne with a woman's body inside. They still haven't identified the body. It could be Clara. They have sent the body to the Reno Coroner's office," explained Winona.

"Has anyone seen the child? Does the Sheriff have any leads as to where she could be?" questioned Maggie.

"No. Bunny just disappeared. I believe someone has her and is keeping her captive. But I've no proof. That's why I need you to find her. I know how you like to solve crimes. Again, this should be right up your alley," Winona explained between sobs.

Maggie thought for a minute, watching the snow falling. "Winona, I'll gladly come to help, but I can't do anything during this snowstorm. According to the weather, it's supposed to snow for two more days or so." Maggie rubbed her chin, "However, I was coming down your way anyway, as I'm writing articles about a few towns around there for a magazine. I needed to review my memory of them, so I will stop by and see you."

"I understand about the snow. I appreciate any help you can give us," replied Winona. Maggie heard a baby cry in the background. "The baby wants to be fed. She is three months old. The whole house is a mess. I can't sleep and think it's affecting my milk as I'm nursing her," sobs Winona.

"Soon as the snow stops, I'll be down. Do you live in the same place?"

"Yes. Thank you, Maggie. I know you'll be able to find my daughter," again sobbed Winona.

"For your sake, I hope she gets home before I come down. But if not, I'll do my best."

"That's all I can ask. Thank you so much. I have to feed the baby. Look forward to seeing you."

After Maggie hung up, she thought, *what did I get myself into? Hope I can find Bunny and she is okay.*

Aaron was concerned their food wouldn't last as the darn snow hadn't stopped for two days. He was thankful for plenty of dry firewood on the porch, which had an overhang to protect it. The other good thing was everyone but Randy had gone camping, so they knew how to rough it.

The girls filled pots with snow, which they melted on the stove for warm water. They found an old dishpan in the sink, which they used for a cat bath. In cleaning the shack, the girls also found some old coffee and tea. So, this gave them something besides the melted snow and apple juice to drink. They even found an old battery-type lamp with a dead battery, some rubber boots, playing cards, and several jigsaw puzzles.

Aaron said, "My dad liked to build the puzzles, and the boots are his. Bet they fit me now." Which they did.

Randy said, "I can charge the battery with the truck battery so we can have some light at night."

"Really," said Rosa.

Aaron wasn't listening. Instead, he said, "I'm not sure how long it will snow. However when it quits, I'm unsure if we can get out of here. The snow is almost two feet deep right now. The way it's coming down, we could get another foot," he told the group. "The biggest problem is food. We are going to have to eat only one meal."

"This is just like camping," Rosa said. "We can stretch what we have for at least a week. We can miss a meal or two as long as we have water. At least that is what my dad used to say."

"Mine too," chimed in the group.

Aaron scratched his head, "I just thought of something. I must be brain-dead. This man was really prepared! You know, we never looked under the tonneau cover on the truck bed. There might be more stuff under there, like tools or a gun."

Randy took the battery to charge it from the truck battery as they ran out the door to the barn, sinking in the snow. Aaron forgot to put the boots on. The girls watched out the window and snickered.

The boys were out of breath when they got to the truck in the barn—pushing back the tonneau cover. Pay dirt! There was an axe, a shovel, a hammer, a battery lantern with a good battery, a large ice chest, and two more bags of food.

Aaron opened the ice chest. It had three packs of hot dogs, three bags of hamburger patties, three gallons of milk, several deli meats, three dozen eggs, and four pounds of bacon. They had hit the jackpot!!

The bags of food contained hamburger and hot dog buns, chips, mustard, ketchup, syrup, pancake mix, and a can opener. There were also a couple of bags of clothes. Where ever the man was going to take them, he definitely was prepared.

Aaron said, "Good thing we found it, or this could have spoiled. Let's drag everything back to the shack."

"And with this light, I don't need to charge the other battery," stated Randy. Aaron just looked at him, unsure what he was talking about.

It took them half an hour to slide the ice chest with bags of food on top to the porch in the snow. After another trip, they got everything to the porch. The boys were soaked and cold when they got in. They stood dripping by the fire, telling the girls what they found. Everyone was excited.

Rosa ran out and started packing the ice chest with snow to keep everything cold. "My mom taught me this when the power goes out during a snowstorm."

"I will shovel a path to the outhouse with the shovel we found. As soon as I warm up," stated Aaron.

Randy took the food from the two big bags and placed them on the counter. Smiling at Rosa, he gave her the can opener, "Just for you."

She laughed, "This will come in handy. It's a lot easier than the spoon trick."

Bunny went and dragged in the bag of clothes. When everything calmed down, Bunny quietly said, "We'll survive; someone will find us if we stay here. We are safe and warm, and now we have food. I've heard of people who left their cars in a snowstorm and died."

They all shook their heads in agreement. However, Aaron hoped someone would find them.

Chapter Six

The man bought a used green Dodge four-wheel drive truck in Yerington. However, he wasn't sure what direction the children had headed. But for some reason, he felt they were still somewhere close. He had listened in the coffee shop to see if anyone had found the kids. Nothing. He did hear they found the burned cabin with a woman's body and a child missing. Everyone had an opinion about that. Probably a domestic was the main thought.

He decided to stay in Hawthorne instead of Yerington. He didn't know why but felt that the kids might be around there, seeing they had escaped from outside of Hawthorne. He knew he had to find those kids before the law did. They watched him kill people to obtain them.

He had removed his fake wig and beard, significantly changing his looks. He didn't want the truck driver to remember that wild man with a beard he picked up around the Hawthorne area and dropped off in Yerington, just in case.

The man figured the kids probably had found all the food. They were now hiding somewhere because of the storm. But where? He didn't understand why they hadn't gone to the authorities, but they were young kids, even if they were smart.

He also thought *the darn truck has a full tank of gas. They could go anywhere, and this snowstorm wasn't helping. They were expecting another ten inches tonight.*

Maggie was looking around on her computer, she loved researching, plus there was nothing to do in this snowstorm. Pete was watching TV.

She was usually gone on Wednesday night to quilt and drink wine. Maggie joined the Wild Stitchers Quilting Club several years ago at the Fabric Chicks in Gardnerville. Over the years, the group has solved several mysteries. In fact, Maggie has become known as the Murder She Wrote lady of Carson Valley.

The group consists of Beth, the owner of Fabric Chicks. She is the youngest, blue eye blond of forty. The rest are in their sixties. Betty Santos, single, with beautiful dyed blond hair, Mary Sorenson, a tiny little lady. Nan Morgan was Maggie's best friend, all 119 lbs. of her and fluffy Maggie. However, tonight, they canceled the quilting class due to the storm.

Maggie, being bored, started reading last week's local newspapers online. What caught her eye in the Fallon paper was six days ago, the authorities found a father dead from a gunshot, and his ten-year-old son was missing.

In the Reno paper, a six-year-old boy was kidnapped from a park in Reno two days later. In the Yerington paper, a young man was found shot to death, and his six-year-old sister was missing. She didn't find any missing children in Carson City's paper.

Missing kids was big news in these smaller towns, except Reno, which always has lots of crime. However, this crime was committed in the daytime in front of other people in a family park.

She thought *this was interesting, three children missing, now Bunny. All happened about two days apart and all about the same age, six and seven, except for the ten-year-old.* Maggie's gut started acting up. *Was this something sinister, like sex trafficking, or were these just random acts of violence?*

Darn snow, now more than ever, she wanted to go to Schurz. Maggie wondered who has the children. Were they kidnapped? Runaway? Doubt it at that age, maybe the ten-year-old. Her mind was going a mile a minute. Her gut was telling her the kidnapping was all related somehow, but how and why?

She had planned to write her articles for the magazine when she went to the different towns, as she would take her tape recorder. There's so much history in that area.

However, to keep her mind busy, she decided to start her article now for the magazine. She was thankful that she knew a lot about the area. There are so many interesting places before Schurz, like Wabuska, Fort Churchill, Mason, Anaconda Mine, and Yerington, but *I will save those for another article.*

**Looking to do something that is off the beaten path?
Visit Schurz, Hawthorne, Luning, Gabbs, Berlin, Ione
Ending up at Middlegate.**

Maggie McDonald

Take a week or make several day trips and travel the back roads to the following mentioned spots. There is hiking, fishing, and spelunking. It's well worth your while to see rural Nevada.

Just a fun piece of trivia, there are fourteen different Mountain ranges located in the state. We may be considered a desert, but that is primarily southern Nevada. In Northern Nevada, the Great Basin National Park is outside of Ely. Mt. Whitney, located there, is the tallest mountain in the "lower 48" states. The elevation at the summit is 14,494.

Nevada is a beautiful State with lots of history, plus it's versatile with Lake Tahoe, many State Parks, a National Park, mining, and agriculture to Sin City=Las Vegas. So, go and enjoy visiting the following places.

Schurz is in Mineral County. It was founded in 1891. The town was named after Carl Schurz, the Secretary of the Interior. Currently, about six hundred and fifty people live there. It's part of the Walker River Indian Reservation, a size of sixty square miles, and the population is mainly Paiute Indians.

Schurz is known for the burial place of Wovoka, who originated the Ghost Dance movement. The Ghost Dance (Natdia) was a spiritual movement created in the late 1869s when conditions were so terrible on Indian reservations that Native Americans needed something to give them hope. This movement was founded by a Paiute Indian named Wovoka, who announced that he was the messiah who came to earth to prepare the Indians for their salvation.

Before the religious movement, a devastating typhoid fever epidemic struck in 1867. This and other European diseases killed approximately one-tenth of the total population, resulting in widespread psychological and emotional trauma to the tribe. This disruption brought disorder to their economic system and society. Many families were prevented from their nomadic lifestyle.

In 1869, Hawthorne Wodziwob, a Paiute man, organized a series of community dances to announce a vision. He spoke of a journey to the land of the dead and promises made to him by the souls of the deceased. They promised to return to their loved ones.

The tribe accepted his vision, likely due to his status as a great healer. He urged the populace to dance the typical circle dance that is customary during a time of celebration. He preached this message with the help of a local "weather doctor" named Tavibo, father of Wovoka.

The Nevada Northern Paiute was the first to practice the Ghost Dance. The practice swept throughout much of the Western States. As the Ghost Dance spread, Tribes established particular ritual aspects with their own Tribal beliefs and needs. It's a very sacred movement honored by all, even today.

Schurz is small but has had a U.S. post office ever since 1891. Schurz is located at the junction of U.S. Route 95 and U.S. Route 95 Alternate. It's around a two-hour drive from Carson City, but well worth a visit.

***

Hawthorne. It was established in 1880, by H. M. Yerington, president of the Carson and Colorado Railroad Co., as a site for the new railroad. Yerington named the town after a friend he knew in Carson City. The first Carson-Colorado train arrived in 1881, carrying prospective buyers to establish the town.

Hawthorne was critical to Knapp's Station and Ferry Landing on the busy Esmeralda Toll Road from Wadsworth to Candelaria. Roads from surrounding mining areas were built to arrive in Hawthorne, mainly because of the railroad.

In 1883, Hawthorne became the county seat, taking it from Esmeralda County due to the town of

Aurora's declining population. They later lost the seat to Goldfield. However, in 1911, it became the county seat for the newly established Mineral County by the Nevada State Legislature. It has been the county seat ever since.

About three thousand people currently live there, year-round. The nearby Hawthorne Army Depot is the primary economic base, which stores all types of ammunition.

"Construction began on Hawthorne Army Depot in July 1928 and received its first shipment of high explosives in October 1930. When the United States entered World War II, the Depot became the staging area for bombs, rockets, and ammunition for almost the entire war effort. Employment was at its highest at 5,625 in 1945. By 1948, the Depot occupied 104 square miles of the 327 square miles under Navy jurisdiction. Subsequently, excess Navy lands were returned to the Bureau of Land Management.

The U.S. Marine Corps provided security for the 3,000 bunkers at the base. On September 1930, and during World War II, 600 Marines were assigned to the facility. In 1977, that number was reduced to 117; security is currently under contract to a private company." From Wikipedia.

It is interesting to see the ammunition bunkers sitting out in the desert. Years back, when they burned off the ammo, you could see the lights from the burn all the way to Virginia City. There was no light pollution as the state was so small in population. The burn looked like the Northern Lights.

When Walker Lake was fuller, the Lunes would come in, and they would celebrate the Lune festival. However, even without the festival, there are lots to see in Hawthorne and enjoy Walker Lake for camping and fishing.

Toward the end of summer, Hawthorne becomes overwhelmed with a little spider that feeds off mosquitoes. They are everywhere, so keep that in mind if you like to camp then.

Visiting for a day or more would be best to see everything Hawthorne offers.

***

Luning An unincorporated town in Mineral County. Luning was an active railroad loading facility for many years. During World War II, magnesium ore from Gabbs was sent to Luning and placed on railroad cars bound for the West. In 1955, the Basic Refractories opened a mine in Gabbs. It produced the magnesium that was trucked to the Luning loading platform. That is where most of the men in Luning at that time worked.

The town once had a small store with an attached gas station, a saloon, a volunteer fire department, a post office, and a one-room school. Everything except the Post Office has closed. A sign in the now-closed Long Branch Saloon says, "Settled 1864." It's often considered a ghost town, but it's not. The population is around eighty hardy people living there year-round.

Moreover, Luning has had two improvements over the last few years. They now have cell service and improved their highway rest area, used by truckers, campers, and people who need a rest, as Luning is on Hwy 95 on the way from Carson City to Las Vegas.

The closest town is Hawthorne, where everyone shops. If you are looking for fast food, this town is lacking. But visit and drive the streets, lots of history. The railroad platforms are still standing. It is about a thirty-minute drive from Hawthorne.

***

Maggie thought that was enough for now. I'll continue when I get down there. Whenever it quits snowing...

The phone rang. It was Nan, Maggie's best friend and quilting partner. "Hi there, lady. What are you doing?" asked Maggie.

"Bored out of my mind. Will this snow ever stop? Bill has been watching the history channel for days," whined Nan. "What are you doing?"

"Working on my magazine article. Well, when the snow quits, you want to take a road trip to

Schurz?" Maggie then told Nan what was happening and what her research had found.

"Will this adventure involve the whole quilting group?" asked Nan.

"I'm not sure, but probably, we've been solving mysteries together. Why not this one?" laughed Maggie.

"I think I can get away for a day or two when this darn snow stops," snickered Nan.

"Then we are on. We'll have to leave the dogs home on this trip. Maybe later we can take them. I feel we'll be making several trips or staying over."

Maggie's dogs are Yazoo, a ten-year-old black Labrador, and fifteen-year-old Murphy, a white Bichon Frise. Nan has Shep, a ten-year-old Border Collie. The dogs are part of their family. Usually, Yazoo and Shep go everywhere they go.

Chapter Seven

After four days, the snow stopped for a bit. The kids got up to a cold, cloudy with the blue sky interjected here and there. They didn't care. They were kids.

They ran to build a snowman and threw snowballs at each other. They had so much energy. Rosa and Bunny made snow angels. They forgot what was going on in their lives. It was just fun being a kid playing in the snow.

Aaron, the serious one, figured they were stuck here for a while, as there were over two feet of snow. Even with the truck's four-wheel drive, it would be tricky with street tires to leave.

There was enough food for at least ten days. But Aaron feared no one was looking for them except the man. The good thing is that he could only get them if he snowshoed in or had aggressive tires on his vehicle, but first, he would have to know where they were hiding.

Rosa's family has a small Mexican restaurant, so she knew a little about cooking. She cooked on an old pan, saving the bacon grease for frying eggs, hamburgers, and hotdogs. Rosa did the cooking on the wood stove. Bunny helped, however, she could, as she didn't know how to cook. She was the smallest of them all.

Randy had never been camping, but he picked up quickly on helping with chores. He loaded the wood pile in the shack and cleaned the stove ashes into an old bucket they had found in the barn.

Arron found some rope in the barn, so he hung it up in the cabin with one of the blankets to give them privacy in taking a cat bath. The bag of clothes fit them, except Aaron, who was tall. The jeans fit around the waist but looked like long shorts. But he thought *they were clean.*

They were like a young family, all getting along to survive. He was mad at himself. He should have gone to the Sheriff's office in Hawthorne, but he had it in his brain to go home. Aaron was the worrywart of the group. However, as of now, things are going well.

With a break in the weather, the man went to the Yerington airport and hired a person with a plane. The man told him he was looking for property to buy and asked if he could fly over different areas to check on some properties listed that were off the grid for sale. They flew up to Wabusa, Yerington, Schurz, and around Hawthorne. Not seeing what he was looking for, mainly his truck. *How far can a ten-year-old drive in the snow? They didn't go to the Sheriff's office or home. He would have heard. Where can they be? These are just kids... but of course, he has to remind himself they're smart kids...apparently smarter than him, as they escaped.*

Maggie called Winona to say she was coming down, "Do you have any new information?"

"No. Nothing," said Winona with stress in her voice. "It's been almost a week that Bunny has been missing. I'm beside myself. The Sheriff said the trail goes cold if they don't find a missing child in the first forty-eight hours. I've been pulling my hair out. No Bunny or Clara. Hank calls every day crying. My world is crazy. I worry about what is happening with my daughter, whether she's alive or a sex toy. Maggie, the mind does terrible things," ranted Winona.

"Well, we will see what we can do, be there in about two to three hours."

"Thank you, see you then."

Maggie thought, *where could Bunny be? Does anyone have her and maybe the other missing kids too? Is there some sex ring out there?*

Darn, her mind was doing what Winona's mind was doing.

Chapter Eight

On her way to Schurz, Maggie picked up Nan, who lived down the street. Nan came out with a basket of goodies. She had made fresh nut bread and had a thermos of coffee. Maggie laughed to herself. *Thank goodness she had brought water.* "You always remember to bring food. Guess that is why I love you." They both laughed.

While driving, Maggie called Mary Sorenson, a Wild Stitchers member on the Jeep's blue tooth. Mary works for the Detective Division in Douglas County Sheriff's Office.

"Hi, Mary. Nan and I are going to Schurz to help a friend whose six-year-old child went missing about a week ago. While researching, I read about three other missing children, two with family members killed and the third child kidnapped. All about the same age, ten to six. Have you guys heard or seen anything on this?"

"Funny you should ask. The Detectives were talking about it this morning. They were all kidnapped or whatever about two days apart. They believe it all could be related, but it's not in our jurisdiction. Is this our new mystery? We have been too quiet. We need some excitement," laughed Mary.

"Okay. This could be a mystery for the club. We have to find those kids," commented Maggie.

"I'll search around here to see what the guys think and let you know if they have any clues."

"Thanks, Mary. I'll let you know what we find out in Schurz. Also, a female from the burned cabin was sent to the Reno Coroner's office. Could you see what you can find out about that? Thanks again for your help."

"Not a problem. I'll get back to you as soon as possible."

Maggie made good time. They arrived after eleven, as there was little traffic, mainly eighteen-wheelers, headed for Las Vegas, as they probably got caught in Reno until the storm passed.

She drove to Winona's house and thought, *I hope we can find Bunny.* She and Nan went to the door and knocked. Winona opened the door quickly and hugged Maggie, "So glad you are here." Maggie could tell the twenty-eight-year-old was under stress with the bags under her eyes. She looked so much older. Her dark hair even had some grey.

"This is Nan. She is also here to help," stated Maggie.

"I appreciate all the help we can get," sobbed Winona. They all went into the big warm kitchen and had a seat. The two boys came running in from the front room.

"My Chad, how you have grown. What are you now, seven? Eight?" asked Maggie.

"Eight. This is Billy, my younger brother. He's four," voiced Chad, smiling.

"The last time I saw Billy, he was just learning to walk. Look at you. Billy," Maggie replied, "You have grown up too, young man." She hugged both boys.

Nan said, "I brought some nut bread," which she took out of her bag. "Would you like some?" Showing the bread to the kids and looking at Winona.

"Yes. They can have a piece." Looking at the boys with a smile. Nan cut them each a slice. After saying thank you, the boys returned to the front room with their treat to watch cartoons on the TV.

"I made some coffee. Do you want some?" As she grabbed three cups from the cupboard. "Yes, please. So, fill us in. Anything new?" asked Maggie.

"Nothing," and Winona started to cry again. Maggie got up and gave her a big hug.

"Well, I may have some info. I did some research, and three other children are missing. They were taken about two days apart from each other." Maggie proceeded to fill Winona in.

"You say two people were murdered, and the kids disappeared. That could only mean the woman they found is Clara." Winona started crying again.

"That means I may have lost my sister as well as my daughter. This is more than I can handle," as she put her hands over her face.

"We aren't sure they are connected, sorry, but my gut thinks so. I have a friend at the Douglas County Sheriff's office looking into it. We'll put the pieces together. Tell me again how Bunny disappeared."

Winona told her the whole story again. "I should have known Clara was up to something but never would believe she would take Bunny." Winona hit her forehead, "If I had called the authorities right away, they might have found Bunny." About then, the baby cried. "I have to feed Lenora," as she got up and entered the bedroom.

Maggie looked at Nan, "Looks like her sister was involved somehow with Bunny's disappearance. Not sure how, but we will figure it out." As she rubs her chin.

Winona came out with the baby in the nursing sling. Maggie said, "Oh, Winona, she is beautiful. The dark hair and almost black eyes."

"She looks like Bunny did at this age. I hope she's as intelligent as Bunny. Bunny is only six but is in second grade and a straight-A student. Her math skills are amazing, and she never forgets... Anything! Her Dad and I don't know where or how she got so smart," Winona again sobbed.

"Before Clara picked up Bunny, did she ever spend any time with her?" asked Nan.

"No. In fact, none of us saw much of Clara because of their drinking. They weren't a lot of fun to be around. Hank has a roving eye and can be a pain in the behind," Winona smiled. "Now he calls every day crying he's broke and would Chad buy him some beer."

"Do you know anyone at the Bureau of Indian Affairs (BIA) that I could talk to, or is the Mineral County Sheriff's office handling the case?" Maggie asked.

"I believe they are working together, seeing they found the body outside of Hawthorne, which is in the Mineral County Sheriff's jurisdiction. However, with an Indian child missing, Tribal

Police are involved. I have a card that Sheriff Deputy Adams gave me with the case number on it. The person at Tribal Police/BIA would be Mike Faris." Winona got up and took the cards off the refrigerator. "Here are the cards with their phone numbers."

Maggie took her cell phone from her pocket and first called the Mineral County Sheriff's Office. She wanted to set up an appointment with Deputy Adams. She lucked out. He would be on shift at three. He could see her then, according to the Secretary. Maggie then called Mike at BIA. No luck there. It was his day off. She left her name and number for him to call.

"It's around one now, so we have time to kill before getting to Hawthorne. If you don't mind, I'm going to nose around town. Clara had to meet someone at some time for her to be where she was if that body was hers. Darn, this is confusing without all the facts. But I'll assume the body is Clara, hoping I'm wrong." Soon as she said that, Winona started crying. Maggie hugged her again, "We'll let you know what we find out."

Maggie and Nan left Winona and started for town. Schurz is not that big. They drove by the school and went to the store.

"Maybe she met the person or people here," said Nan.

"It is possible. Then again, Clara could have met them at a bar in Hawthorne," stated Maggie.

Chapter Nine

Maggie and Nan went into the convenience store. There was an older, heavyset lady behind the counter. She didn't smile when they came in. Maggie walked up to her with her hand out to shake, "Hi. I'm Maggie McDonald, a good friend of Winona Malone. I'm here helping her to find Bunny and Clara."

The woman never changed expression and left Maggie's hand hanging. "I told Winona all I knew. Never saw either one of them that day."

"Yep, that's what Winona said, but I was curious if Clara talked to anyone before that day," replied Maggie.

The woman seemed to warm up a bit. She thought for a moment. "You know, a couple of days before Clara and Bunny disappeared, I saw her talking to a guy while they were pumping gas. I had never seen him before."

"Might mean something. What did he look like?" asked Maggie.

"If I remember right, he was tall and skinny with wild-looking brown hair and a long brown beard. But he wasn't old as he walked too fast. You know he paid with a credit card. Give me a moment." She walked into the back room.

Maggie and Nan thought maybe they got a lead as they waited. A few minutes later, she came out with a handful of receipts. Placing them on the counter, she started going through them. "Here we go," as she holds up the receipt. "The name on the credit card is listed as George Fuller."

Maggie thought for a moment. *She had heard that name before, but where?* "Thanks so much for your help. I will pass this on to the authorities," Maggie put her hand out again to say thank you, and this time the lady shook it.

Maggie and Nan returned to the Jeep and headed for Hawthorne to meet with Deputy Adams.

"That was interesting," sighed Nan.

"I am not sure that's his real name. My memory tells me I heard or read that name somewhere."

It was almost three when they pulled up to the Sheriff's office. Going in, they saw an officer behind the counter and asked to see Deputy Adams. "Have a seat, and I'll send him out."

The wall behind the officer was lined with filing cabinets and bulletin boards. The office had an air of efficiency and looked very professional.

Ten minutes later, the deputy came out. "I'm Deputy Adams. How can I help you, ladies?"

"Well, I'm hoping we can help you. This has to do with the missing child Bunny Malone," stated Maggie.

He looked at them momentarily and said, "Come back to a room." They followed him. There was a table with four chairs and a two-way mirror when they entered the room. After everyone was seated, he offered coffee.

Nan laughed, "No thanks, it's jail coffee, but will take some water."

"Been in jail before," he laughed. He smiled as he went and got three bottles of water. When he returned, "Now, what do you know about this case?"

Maggie gave him one of her cards and filled him in on what they knew and the name of the man seen talking to Clara, which could be nothing. "Winona asked me to look into this mess, as we have been friends for years. You can check on me with the Douglas County Sheriff's Office, Detective Division. They know me as we have helped with a few crimes."

"I'll be back," taking her card, he left the office. Maggie and Nan sat there drinking their water when Maggie's cell phone rang.

"Hi." It was Mary. "What kind of trouble are you guys in?" she asked, laughing.

"We are sitting in the interview room at the Mineral County Sheriff's office, trying to help. I guess he called you guys to check on us."

"Yep."

"Did you find anything out about what we discussed this morning?"

"Not much. The coroner still hasn't identified the body. However, I have the names of the victims and missing kids. Aaron Fuller, 10, is from Fallon, and his Dad, George Fuller, was killed. Randy Ward, 6, was kidnapped in Reno in front of people. They did get a description of the suspect. He was tall and skinny, with wild brown hair and a long brown beard. The third victim, Rosa Sanchez, 7, is from Yerington. Her brother Mario Sanchez was killed. Then Bunny Malone, which you know about."

"Interestingly, we found out Clara was seen talking to a man you describe in Ward's kidnapping. Plus, he used George Fuller's credit card for gas. I think these crimes are all related. The million-dollar question is, why he kidnapped them, and where are the kids now?" queried Maggie.

Deputy Adams came back into the room with a smile. "You are an interesting lady, and I would love your help."

"Now that we have established that, what is your first name?" asked Maggie, laughing.

"Rex. Rex Adams."

Maggie laughed again and filled him in on what she learned. It was decided that they would work together. The main thing was to find these kids. At least they had a description of the man.

However, they needed more to go on. Maggie asked Rex if they could draw a picture of a tall skinny guy with wild hair and a long beard. Someone may remember seeing him even if he had shaved and cut his hair.

"Yes, we have an artist in the department. That is a good idea," replied Adams. "We can post it in different places and the newspaper."

"We might get lucky," said Nan.

Chapter Ten

It had been raining hard for an hour or so. Now it was back snowing big wet flakes, so everything was icy. Aaron thought *we'll never get out of here if this keeps up. The food can't last forever. I must set a trap for rabbits or whatever is running around. I have to catch some meat.*

Aaron said, very concerned, "We must cut back to one meal a day unless I can trap something more to eat. Randy, you and I have to gather fallen wood for the fire. We have been here almost two weeks, and no one has found us. We aren't sure anyone is even looking for us except the man."

Rosa said, "I can stretch the food for another week or better." As she was doing all the cooking.

Bunny looks up, "If we keep bundled, we can cut the fire down. Even though the shack's not insulated, it'll stay above freezing. The snow drifts are helping to keep the heat in, like an igloo. That will save on wood.

"That's a good idea," said Randy. We have a shovel. I'll pile more snow on the side that doesn't have drifts."

"But food is still the issue," said Aaron. "I'll start building some traps. I have the axe and hammer. I'll see if there are any nails in the barn." Aaron wore his dad's rubber boots and a jacket and headed for the barn. The snow was deep, still over two feet, even after the rain.

Aaron thought as he looked for nails. *The man was so prepared, can't believe he didn't have a gun or something.* So, he started searching the cab of the truck. Found a cell phone in the console. It still had a charge of less than twenty percent. But no bars for cell service. *That's no good.* He put it in his back pocket. Aaron pushed the back seats up as there was storage space back there. *Wow.* He found a 22 rifle, bullets, and a hunting knife.

He looked in the glove compartment and found the truck was recently purchased. *That explained why there were no license plates.* The name listed as the owner was George Fuller, *his dad.* He started to cry. He hadn't cried since his dad was killed. *The man killed his dad and stole his identity too.*

The man was drinking coffee at the local restaurant when he spotted the paper. On the front page was a drawing of him, not a good one, but he could be recognized.

Darn, where did they get this concept? He was glad he had removed his fake wig and beard. Somehow the law has figured the person in the drawing was behind all the missing kids. *Wonder where I slipped up?*

The man was beside himself as now the law was putting things together. It had been two weeks, and nothing new about the kid's whereabouts. *And darn, it was snowing again.* The kids have to be out of food. Maybe they had a wreck and died.

Hopefully, that didn't happen. His mind was swirling.

He had planned this project for over six months and didn't want to lose those kids. He thought, *do I give it another week, then cut my losses, or do I find them before the law finds them or me? But darn, where do I look?* He was not a happy camper as he rubbed his chin. Things were not going the way he had planned.

Maggie was looking out the kitchen window, drinking her coffee, watching it snow again. *Would this winter ever end?* Her gut was telling her she needed to find those kids soon. She believed they were all together, but where would he hide them? It could be anywhere. She had a picture in her mind of what he looked like now. She figured he had shaven and most definitely cut his hair.

She also was under pressure to finish her magazine article. The weatherperson said the snow should stop tomorrow, hopefully, with a couple-day break. Maybe she could kill two birds with one stone by finishing her story and finding the kids.

So tomorrow, she was going back down to Schurz, then Hawthorne, and if she had time to Gabbs. She started packing a little overnight bag. She was going to stay in Hawthorne for a couple of days. Pete didn't want to go, so he would stay home and care for the dogs.

Yazoo knew something was up. "I'm sorry guys, but you and Murphy will stay with Dad," she hugged them. Nan was going to go with her.

Chapter Eleven

Bang! Bang! The kids huddled together in fear. Thinking the man must have found them.

The shack door opened, and it was Aaron. Aaron came in carrying a rabbit. He was smiling from ear to ear. "We will have meat. I found a gun and a hunting knife."

"You scared us. We thought the man had found us," Randy said excitedly.

"I'm sorry didn't mean to scare you." Then he proceeded to tell them what he had found. Aaron took the rabbit and started cleaning and skinning it with the hunting knife.

"I have cooked rabbit before at the restaurant," explained Rosa. "We had an old man who would bring them in for us to cook for him."

"Let me see the cell phone," asked Randy reaching for it.

Aaron handed it to him, "But there's no cell service."

"I want to see who owned the phone. If it's your dad's, we can leave a text message where we are," explained Randy.

"How can you do that with no service?" asked Aaron.

"I don't know, but I am good at working with phones. I can probably get us cell service if I find the right stuff in the barn. Then we can send a text." After playing with it for a couple of minutes, "The phone belonged to Mario Sanchez, Rosa's brother," explained Randy.

"Let me see," asked Rosa. She hit pictures, and there was her family. She started to cry, "Yep, this is his."

Randy went to type where they were, but he didn't know. Aaron knew the area but wasn't sure either.

Bunny popped up and said, "Here are the directions." She rattled them off to Randy. "Hwy 361, climb the Galavada Pass, which is over the 6500-foot summit, and one mile on the downside, turn left, go two miles to the line shack."

Randy said as he typed the information into the phone. "Now I have to get cell service."

Everyone looked at each other and realized they all had above-average intelligence. Aaron thought as he looked around. *Maybe this is why the man wanted us.*

Bunny said, "I may be six, but I'm in the second grade. I'm good at math and have a memory that never forgets."

Rosa said, "We are going to be saved. My talent is art. I can tell the law what the man looked like down to the mole on his hand and that his hair and beard were fake. I'm like Bunny. I never forget details."

Randy said excitedly, "I need to make an antenna. The antenna will pick up a weak signal from the nearest cell tower, amplify and direct the signal where needed. This mountain is high, and I believe there was a cell tower in Luning. I may have to get on the roof, but first, I must build the antenna."

Randy started looking through the cabin and found a long-handled spoon. "I need some wire." Looking at Aaron, "Let's go to the barn. There's bound to be some bailing wire in the straw." The two boys went trudging out into the snow to the barn.

Randy looked around in the straw and found some bailing wire. "This should work."

When they returned to the shack, Randy took the back off the phone and inserted the wire in the external antenna hole. He held the phone up. It had one bar that bounced. Everyone got excited.

"I have to get up higher," stated Randy.

Aaron said, "Let me try. I am taller."

"First, let's wire the phone to the spoon and then reach as far as you can," directed Randy.

Aaron did as he was told and reached as high as he could, standing on the bed. "It looks like we got 2 bars."

"We can send a text or call 911 with two bars. I already typed out the text to my dad. Just push send," replied Randy.

The text when through. The phone was almost dead. It was below five percent.

"Now, let's try calling 911." Bringing the phone down, Randy typed in the text to 911 and had Aaron push sent as he stood on the bed. "Hopefully, it went through, and I hope the phone has GPS."

"Now we wait to see if anything went through," sighed Randy.

Chapter Twelve

Dick Ward was sitting in his recliner, getting drunk. It had been over two weeks since his son was kidnapped. Dick hadn't shaved in a week and was wearing sweats. Randy's birthday was next week, and his son was still missing or worse. He couldn't get over the pain he felt. He didn't want to think he would never see his son again. He had another swig of the stiff drink with tears in his eyes.

His phone beeped, saying he was receiving a text from Randy. *Damn, is this a cruel joke? Who would text this kind of information? They must know he was kidnapped. It was in the paper.* This text says they are down by Luning. *Where in the heck is Luning?* He was abducted weeks ago in Reno. *Darn Scammers.*

Dick texted back, "Not nice. Cruel joke, butt heads." As he threw the phone and sobbed.

The cell beeped a message. Randy read it as the phone died. "Dad didn't believe the message," cried Randy.

Randy then grabbed the battery from the working light, wrapped the bailing wire around the post, and took the battery out of the phone. He wrapped the wire around it to get a charge. "I am going to try this. If it doesn't work, we will try the truck battery to charge the phone battery. It will take a while."

Everyone watched in amazement.

Seeing it started snowing again, but lightly, Maggie and Nan were bored. The weather had said there would be a break in the storm. Well, it hadn't happened yet. She and Nan were stuck in the motel room in Hawthorne. Nan was taking a nap. Maggie was at her computer writing her article when she got this hair-brained idea. She decided to call the families of the missing kids. She called Deputy Rex Adams, "Hi Rex, this is Maggie. I want to talk to the different families involved in this mess. Can you help me?"

"Wow, they are in different jurisdictions, but let me see what I can do. What are you looking for?"

"Winona said something the other day about how smart Bunny is in math and never forgets details. I wonder if all these kids are super smart. That might be the connection and why the man kidnapped them."

"I'll look into it and get back to you."

"Thanks. Let me know what you find out."

That wasn't what Maggie wanted to hear. *She wanted to talk to the families. Well, let's see what Google gives me.* She typed in Randy Ward, and a picture popped up of the young man with red hair, talking about him getting an award for resolving a phone lock program, saving a company thousands of dollars. *Interesting, and he's six.*

The next name she typed in was Rosa Sanchez. She was a noted artist at seven. Her work is on display at the Nevada Museum of Arts in Reno as one of the youngest artists.

The third name was Aaron Fuller. A picture appeared with him showing medals. He earned gold medals in 4H shooting sports. *Pete would love that. In fact, he may know him.* Aaron was an excellent basketball player and golfer. At ten, he had won a scholarship to a college of his choice for golf. Plus, being a straight-A student.

So, all the children were overachievers and highly intelligent. If that was the reason for the kidnapping, what did he plan on doing with them? And where are they now? It's been over two weeks. Are they still alive? Maggie's gut felt they were.

Looking out the window, the snow had stopped. Blue skies were trying to break through. Maggie had a gut feeling about going to Luning, and she didn't know why? She yelled at Nan, "Let's drive down to Luning for my article and maybe up to Gabbs, seeing the snow has stopped for a bit.

Nan woke and stretched, "Okay, sounds good. Glad the snow stopped," as she yawned.

Chapter Thirteen

The man thought, *Darn, I have to find those kids. I need to think like them. They are hiding out somewhere, but why? They could have gone to the authorities. Maybe they went to one of the families, and they aren't saying anything. I've met the fathers of the kids. Of course, they don't know me. It was sad that I had to kill Aaron's father, but he was a piece of garbage, a big drunk. He didn't deserve a child like Aaron. I'm not sorry I killed Mario or Clara. They didn't deserve to live. Anyone that would sell their family members doesn't deserve to live.*

These families were blessed to have these kids. They are an asset to this world. I just wanted them to be mine! I could make them rich and be in history books. Darn, where are they? I have to start looking, but in which direction?

The man sat and thought, *Aaron is driving, so where would he go? Not too far in a snowstorm. The Bunny incident happened outside of*

Hawthorne. Maybe they went to Luning or Mina instead of heading toward Schurz. His mind was thinking. *I'm going to drive down to Luning and check it out, as it has quit snowing for now.*

Aaron was glad the snow had stopped for at least a while. Randy was working on charging the phone battery. It was at three percent, and they needed at least five.

"Be patient, maybe another hour. Let's hope the lamp battery doesn't go dead. If it does, we'll try the trucks," said Randy calmly.

Everyone took advantage of the weather break, bringing in more downed wood from the forest. Aaron used the axe to cut the branches to fit in the stove. Randy cleaned the ashes from the stove.

The girls had melted snow earlier and were washing clothes to hang on the rope. They had no soap, just water, but it freshened the clothes. When they got done with their chores, Rosa started frying the rabbit.

Hopefully, they will be able to call for help soon.

Deputy Sheriff Adams talked to the families and learned all the kids were overachievers. But the most exciting item was what Dick Ward had to say about a text he received, supposedly from Randy, saying he was down by Luning. Dick Ward thought it was a cruel joke. However, Rex felt it was worth looking into.

Seeing a break in the snow, he took off and headed down to Luning with the location information from Mr. Ward.

Maggie said, "Hopefully, the road to Gabbs will be clear. There are two steep passes on the way. Not sure if they maintain this road in the snow."

"What is Gabbs known for?" asked Nan.

"Here is part of my article for the magazine. You can read it and tell me what you think," as Maggie pulled the crumbled paper out of her purse.

Gabbs A company town for Basic Magnesium, Inc. (BMI), created in December 1941. It was opened as a magnesium production plant in the area. The town was an earlier mining camp named Brucite, then renamed after the Gabbs Valley and paleontologist William Gabb.

Due to World War II demand for magnesium, the plant expanded under the direction of the War Production Board. The police station, a jail, and a school district were built in 1942. In 1945 Gabbs had a population of over four hundred. Several of the town sections merged, including a library, City Hall, parks, tennis courts, and local newspapers.

In 1944 the magnesium plant closed, having produced enough ore to meet the needs of the war. The population dropped but was revived when a new plant started producing magnesium for the private sector in 1955. The town's population climbed enough for the city to become incorporated.

In 1982 half its workers were laid off, and the town declined. Then in the 1990s, workers came to work at a gold mine nearby Paradise Peak, again expanding the population. Then that plant closed in 1994. In 2001 Gabbs lost its incorporated status. Today the town has a high school, stores, and homes. You can still see the magnesium plant. It is on the road to the Berlin-Ichthyosaur State Park. So, stock up on food and drinks to picnic at the Park.

"Not bad. I didn't know it was such a new town. I think it might make people visit on their way to the State Park," said Nan.

"Thank you. Well, we are coming into Luning. Sadly, this town is dying." She pulled into the rest stop as her blue-tooth phone rang. It was Deputy Adams. "Hey, your idea to contact the families may have paid off. Dick Ward received a text from Randy about where the kids might be. He thought it was a cruel joke. But it may be a lead."

"Wow. Where are the kids located?" asked Nan.

"Outside Luning going to Gabbs. On the downside of the first pass, about one mile, turn left and take a dirt road two miles back. I'm on my way."

"Well, we're in Luning now at the rest stop and finally just got cell service," replied Maggie, "we'll head up. I have a Jeep."

"I'm in a four-by-four truck, so we should be able to make the off-road. Wait for me. I'm just leaving Hawthorne. Hope to be there in twenty minutes."

"Wow. I hope this is a good lead and they are all okay. What about the man?" stated Maggie.

"That's why you need to wait for me, in case there's a problem."

"Good point. Although I have a gun, I've a CCW, my concealed weapons permit."

"Ha-ha, of course, that figures. But still, wait for me to lead."

Chapter Fourteen

The man saw the cop zoom by him outside of Hawthorne with flashing lights, headed for Luning. *I hope that's not a bad sign and that they found the kids.*

Maggie and Nan didn't talk. They just sat with their fingers crossed, praying they would find the kids and all were okay. Maggie's mind was going a mile a minute. *I hope this is for real and we find them.*

It seemed forever before the Sheriff's truck pulled into the rest stop. He waved at them and started going as they followed.

The man pulled into the rest stop as the Sheriff and a Jeep with two women were leaving. *Wondering what is going on? I'll sit here and wait to see.*

Maggie noticed the green truck pull into the rest stop as they were leaving. It didn't have a license plate. But papers were in the window, so the person had just bought the truck. The young man was blond. She wasn't sure why her gut growled.

They drove down Hwy 95, then turned right on Hwy 361 and climbed the Galavada Pass, which s over 6500 feet. The road had been plowed but was icy. About a mile down on the left was a dirt road with a good four-foot berm from the plow, then it looked like it tapered off to around three feet of snow on the road. Both vehicles went into four-by-four as the vehicles had aggressive tires that could handle the snow. The truck plowed the way as he was higher. Slowing down to less than five miles per hour, they followed what they figured was the road.

It seemed like forever to travel the two miles, but as they came around a bend, there was a line shack with smoke coming out of the chimney.

Maggie started tooting her horn to let them know someone was there. After she did that, she thought, *what if the man came out shooting? Not the smartest thing I did.*

However, it was Aaron that came out of the shack with a rifle, ready to protect themselves. He saw the Jeep and the Sheriff's car and started crying. Yelling at the kids, "We are saved! Come outside!" Three little people came out, jumping up and down.

Before leaving the Jeep, Maggie tried to send a message to Winona, but there was no cell service. *How did the kids get a message out?* Maggie hustled over in the deep snow to Bunny, hugging her. "Your mom has been beside herself. Are you guys all okay?"

"We are now," replied Aaron. Everyone was hugging each other. Because of the cold, they all walked into the shack, still hugging each other. The shack smelled nice from good food and was warm. Rosa had been frying rabbit.

"Wow," said Rex, "You guys are true survivors."

"We each have unique talents," explained Rosa. The kids all laughed.

"Well, grab whatever you are taking, and let's get out of here before it starts to snow again," advised the deputy.

"I'll take the girls with me." Bunny was still hugging Maggie. "You can tell us about your adventure on the way back to the Sheriff's office."

When they returned down to Hwy 95, Maggie looked toward the rest stop to see if the green truck was still there. She couldn't see from where she was, but her gut growled.

All the way to Hawthorne, the girls never stopped talking. They had witnessed a lot for such young people.

Rosa said, "He doesn't have long hair and a beard. They were phony. He is young and has blond hair."

"How do you know that, Rosa?" asked Nan.

"I am an artist with a photographic memory. He also has a wart on his hand."

"We will tell the sheriff that when we get there." Maggie thought *the man in the green pickup was blond.* Her gut growled again. Maybe Rosa could draw a picture of him.

"How did you guys survive this long in the shack?" asked Nan.

The girls proceeded to tell them everything, even the about the outhouse.

Maggie and Nan laughed.

Maggie thought. *The kids would need counseling. They have been through so much.*

The man was parked on a side street and saw them come down the road with people in the vehicles. Darn it, they found the kids. *But how? Well, the good thing is the kids don't know what I really look like. Darn, six months of hard work down the drain. Plus, I killed three people for*

nothing. Now I have to start over... or maybe, I can get them back.

Chapter Fifteen

When they all got to the Sheriff's Office, Maggie called Winona. "We have Bunny, and she's in good shape. Will bring her home in a couple of hours. Have to do the paperwork."

"Oh, thank goodness. I knew you would find her. Thank you," as she sobbed.

"All the kids are okay. We are calling the families now. See you in a bit."

"I can't wait to hug my pumpkin and hear how you found them. Thanks. Thank you so much," as she sobbed again, hanging up.

After hearing the kid's stories and having Rosa sketch the man, Rex said he would publish and post.

Rosa also said, "I think my family met the man. He may have come into the restaurant."

Rex asked the other kids if they had seen the man before, showing them Rosa's drawing.

Randy said, "He looks like a man that works in my dad's company. But I'm not sure. My dad would surely know."

Everyone else said they had never seen him before. It took a couple of hours to complete the paperwork.

Nan went and bought everyone tacos and Cokes. Being typical kids, they said they were tired of hot dogs and hamburgers. Maggie laughed.

Rosa's mother and dad from Yerington were the first to arrive to pick her up. Tears were everywhere. Randy's dad was on the way from Reno. Aaron's mother didn't drive as she was disabled, so Aaron's brother, Floyd, was coming from Fallon to pick him up. The kids were tired, as the adrenaline had finally worn off. Bunny had fallen asleep in the chair.

Maggie thought *they had to find this man.* She was afraid he would repeat whatever reason he had to make the kids rich, and he could kill more people. Or worse yet, try to kidnap the kids again.

Seeing they had found the kids and after they completed the paperwork, Maggie took Bunny home. Winona wanted to hear how they found her. Bunny, Maggie, and Nan told Winona and Chad Sr. the story.

Chad Jr. and Billy were happy to have Bunny back home. Maybe life could return to normal, and Mom would be happy again. After an hour or so, Maggie and Nan left the joyous family.

Maggie and Nan decided to spend another night in Hawthorne, so they would travel to the Berlin State Park tomorrow. Then to Middlegate and home. Maggie needed to finish her magazine article. She called Pete to tell him what was going on. Nan called Bill to fill him in. The guys didn't mind.

The man thought he would still hang around in Hawthorne. He wanted to hear how they found the children. Plus, if there was anything he needed to know. If he is lucky, maybe, he could get a couple of them back.

The next day, the newspaper told about the rescue story and a picture of someone looking like him who had kidnapped them. He pulled his hat down. *I will have to dye my hair or wear a different wig.*

In reading the story, he found that Randy made the cell phone work to receive cell service—darn smart kids. He would like to catch Randy and Bunny again... maybe.

Chapter Sixteen

The following day, Maggie and Nan took advantage of the break in the storm and headed to Berlin State Park. It had been a while since either one had been out there.

"I'm not sure they are doing tours of the Diana mine anymore. I had heard they had shut it down," stated Maggie.

Getting to the Park was a chore as they were limited in what they could see because of all the snow. They visited the Ichthyosaur fossil museum and some buildings and talked to the Park Ranger who lived there. After spending a few hours there, Maggie learned some new information about the Park.

"Seeing we're so close," Maggie suggested, "Let's go to Ione."

Nan replied, "I have never been there, so I'm game."

Pulling into Ione, they hit the combination market-bar for water and something to eat. Maggie brought in her computer and started writing her article while they ate.

The Berlin Historic District includes the ghost town of Berlin in Nye County. It made the National Register of Historic Places in 1971. Berlin was created in 1897 as part of the Union Mining District with the opening of the Berlin Mine. It was named for Berlin, Germany, as many of the prospectors came from there. The town never prospered like Tonopah or Goldfield. Berlin was abandoned by 1911.

People would hike the Union Canyon and gather Ichthyosaur fossils. Nevada finally acquired the site in 1970, making it the Berlin–Ichthyosaur State Park to protect the Ichthyosaur fossils.

The Park is on the edge of Toiyabe National Forest at about 6,676 ft. above sea level. The forest above the town becomes more dense, providing the town's building materials. At its peak, about seventy-five buildings and three hundred residents lived there. Berlin was a company town owned by a Nevada Company until the state acquired it in 1970.

The town of Union, one mile away east, was the suburbs of Berlin. With three miles of tunnels, the Berlin Mine produced less than one million dollars of gold and silver. The Diana Mine was the Parks mining museum. However, tours of the mine stopped in 2007 because of safety.

The buildings active in Berlin include the mine supervisor's house, now the park office, the assay office, and a machine shop. The 30-stamp mill was rebuilt, one of the state's best of its type. There is a museum to see the Ichthyosaur fossils. Nevada is the only state that has these fossils. Just reasonably, Paleontologist feels this may have been a birthing place for these fishes. In fact, it's the Nevada State fish.

The Park is mainly dry camping. However, they do provide bathrooms and water in the summer. Warning if you have dogs, there are snakes and coyotes. It's a great place to visit in early or late summer, as it gets mighty hot in mid-summer. Good hiking trails and a fun place to visit. A must-see State Park. Come and stay awhile.

***

Ione is the closest thing to being a ghost town in Nye County, located a few miles from the State Park.

Ione was founded in November 1863 when silver was discovered by P. A. Havens in the Shoshone Range. While the mining in the Union Mining District was closer to Union and Grantsville, Ione became a trade and milling center.

Community members petitioned the territorial government to form a new county, and in January 1864, Nye County became part of the Nevada Territory. Ione was granted a stipend of $800 to construct the county's first courthouse.

The development at Belmont, however, drew away Ione's population. In February 1867, the county seat relocated to Belmont.

Ione's second boom was in 1896 when E. W. Brinell built a new 10-stamp mill. In 1897, A. Phelps Stokes came to the Union District and bought most of the mining and milling interests, further facilitating Ione's resurrection. However, in July 1898, the silver value dropped, and Ione suffered again.

1912 the town saw another growth spurt when cinnabar deposits were found. This material was made into liquid mercury for hard rock mining. This boom was again short-lived, ending in 1914, although the recovery of cinnabar persisted in the district until the 1930s.

With the current population of forty people, not much remains open to the public. Ione's post office closed in 1959, and all remaining businesses have ceased except for the market-bar.

A fun fact: Tremors, the 1990 American western monster film featuring Kevin Bacon, was filmed in Ione! There is a lot of agriculture thanks to the Reese River.

In the 1970s, Hugh Marshall purchased most of the town and twenty-four square miles surrounding it. He also owns the mineral rights. Anyone interested in exploring ghost towns, Ione is definitely one to add to the list!

****

Nan took a swig of her water and started reading. When she finished, she said, "Interesting, I have learned a lot about this area. Sad that it hasn't grown more."

"Many of these counties can't grow as the Bureau of Land Management (BLM) owns the land. In fact, over eighty percent of Nevada is owned by BLM. They give away our State fish fossils to other states. Round up and kill our wild horses and burros. It is time for them to leave and return our land to the state," said Maggie sadly.

Chapter Seventeen

Nan suggested a few changes to Maggie's story. Maggie didn't even comment, yay or nay, to Nan's suggestions, as her mind was elsewhere. Her gut was really bothering her.

"Let's go back to Hawthorne. I've got a feeling about the man. I'm afraid he will try to steal the kids again. I'm not sure why I have this feeling. But he knew these kids from somewhere and selected them."

"You could be right. Randy said he thought he worked with his dad," stated Nan.

"Rosa thought he had been in their restaurant. Darn, anything is possible. We need to bring in the Wild Stitchers so they can keep an eye on the kids."

"How will you do that, as the kids all live so far apart?"

"I'm not sure, but I'm thinking of something. Let's talk to Rex."

It was almost dark when they returned to Hawthorne, but Maggie had called Rex, and they decided to meet at the El Capitan at six thirty. Maggie had a hair-brain idea. They parked in front and went into the restaurant. Rex was already there and had a table. He was in uniform, so he must still be on duty. Maggie and Nan slid into the booth across from him.

"What's up, ladies?" he asked.

"I'm worried about the man trying to kidnap the kids again. He selected those four for a reason. I don't know what his sick mind had planned, but he planned it just the same. He planned everything. The kids said there were food, tools, and clothes. So wherever he was going to take them, he was prepared."

"So what is your point? Or maybe I should say what's your plan?" as he smiled.

"What if we have all the kids come back to Hawthorne to talk about how smart they were to fool this man and escape? We could have the media there, but little police presence that is seen. I think he will come in with guns blazing to take them," Maggie laughed.

"The children would be televised, sort of like Zoom." She explained what she was thinking. "I haven't worked out all the details. But we must do it quickly and protect everyone," commented Maggie. She proceeded to give him the details of her plan.

"Wow," as he rubbed his head. "It's crazy enough that it might work."

"I want to set it up for tomorrow evening if we can. We still have a break in the snow for a few more days, and for some reason, I feel he is still in the area. I've talked to Winona and Rosa's mother and dad. They are open to it. The main reason even the parents don't want the kids to live in fear that he will try to retake them."

"You are right. I feel he will try again. If he killed to get them the first time, he wants those kids," stated Rex. "Oh, also, we got the report from the Reno Coroner's Office. The burned woman was Clara."

"I suspected that, seeing the kids said he shot her in front of them," stated Maggie. "Does Winona know? Never mind, Bunny probably told her the man shot Clara."

"We just got the information. But I am sure BIA will officially inform her."

The three sat and discussed the pros and cons of their plan. Rex said he would call the other parents. They finally felt they had devised a reasonable plan, but anything can always go wrong. They decided to put it in the morning paper that the kids would talk to the media tomorrow night.

After their meeting, Maggie called Beth and Betty to come to Hawthorne that night or first thing in the morning. Beth was to set up the cameras for the Zoom, and Betty would pretend to be the media spoke person and ask the children questions.

The following morning the man was sitting in the coffee shop when he saw the paper about all the kidnapped kids returning to speak to the media. Their story and rescue were big news. They would talk to the press in a conference room at the El Capitan, which was not open to the public, mainly for their security.

He had dyed his hair auburn, so he didn't look like the picture from the other day. He even dyed his eyebrows. *I am glad I hung around. I may get those kids back yet. I would like them all, but I don't need them, just Randy and Bunny.*

So, he prepared to capture them for the rest of the day. He bought food and went to the thrift store for kids' clothes and stuff. He still had the place to hide them. He had a plan up his sleeve on how he would recapture them...

By noon everything was in place. Betty had a script for the questions. Everything would be videoed. They set up a table with four chairs in the conference room on a stage for the kids. The table on stage had TV monitors and one on the table on the floor for Betty.

Everything was prepared. Maggie and Nan had their fingers crossed as it had to work. Beth said it would work. She had done this before at Fabric Chicks with guest speakers. So knowing techie, Beth, this would work.

Chapter Eighteen

The time came for the meeting. Beth had double-checked everything. It was a go. Deputy Brown was placed outside the door as the forum was closed.

Aaron was the first child to talk. He answered Betty's questions. The deputy could hear part of the conversation through the outside door.

As the deputy sat there, a long-legged, good-looking blonde in black leggings came walking down the hall. "Sorry, ma'am, but the hall is closed off."

"But why? What is going on?" she coyly asked.

"The press is interviewing the kidnapped kids," he responded, smiling.

She started to walk by him. "Ma'am, as I said, the hall is closed." She turned and sprayed him in the face with perfume. Then she hit him on the head twice with her purse as he grabbed his eyes from the spray and knocked him out. Quickly, she zip-tied his hands behind him, took his gun, and put a gag in his mouth. She leaned toward the door and listened carefully to see if they had heard any of the noise. She could still hear Aaron talking, so things were still a go.

She opened the door quietly, threw in a smoke bomb, and quickly shut it so it could do its job. She hopes to grab at least two of the kids. She had chloroform and the officer's gun and would take the two down the hall and out the back door. If she were lucky, she would capture them all. She had the truck waiting.

Waiting a few minutes, she took a mask out of her purse and entered the room. She was looking around. *What the heck? There is no one in here. Everybody is on TV. Damn, it's a trap.*

As she turned to leave, five officers were waiting for her by the door. They also were wearing masks. They had watched everything on video. Looking around, and seeing there was no escape in the room. She reached for the gun in her purse.

The officers yelled, "Don't do it! Put the gun down."

She didn't and pointed it at them. Before she could shoot, two of the officers shot her, shooting her in the gun-hand and her right shoulder.

She yelled, "You shot me! You pigs shot me!!!"

She was bleeding but would live. They quickly cuffed her, and in doing so, her wig fell off. "Well, I will be darned if she isn't a he," said one of the officers.

Rosa yelled on the TV, "Check for a wart on his left hand."

The officers did. "He has one," replied the officer.

"That's the man who killed my brother."

The man dropped his head, knowing it was over. Then he yelled in frustration, "I could have made you rich. You just needed to stay with me."

About then, the paramedics arrived and took the man to the ambulance with Deputy Brown to the hospital for their injuries.

Back at the Sheriff's Office, the Sheriff, Rex, Nan, Maggie, Beth, and Betty discussed what had occurred.

"I can't believe we pulled it off," said Rex. "The best part is we have it all on video. Though I never thought he would come for the kids as a woman. He was one deranged man. We discovered by his fingerprints that his name is Joseph James Corona, 36, from Reno. He had a rap sheet for theft and had worked for Tesla. They fired him eight months back."

"Wonder what he meant? He would make the kids rich?" asked Beth.

"We will probably never know for sure. He said something about their DNA. He has to be mentally ill and hopefully will be in prison for a long time," stated Rex.

"So now the kids can go back to living their lives without fear," Maggie sighed.

"We couldn't have done it without the help of the Wild Stitchers," said the Sheriff.

"High five to Beth and Betty." Everyone agreed. Rex smiled, "It was a pleasure working with you gals. I thought it was a crazy idea, but the kids were never in danger, as it was all done on video. Now I know why Douglas speaks so highly of you ladies."

"Beth is the techie of the bunch. Thanks to her, it worked. Couldn't have done it without her. Thanks, Rex, for going along with the scheme," said Maggie.

"Speaking of getting along, we best be heading out," sighed Betty. Everybody hugged everyone as Beth and Betty headed home.

Nan and Maggie were leaving in the morning. "Well, wonder what our next adventure will be?" asked Nan

"If we don't get home to our husbands and fur babies soon, we may find out." They all laughed.

Chapter Nineteen

Maggie and Nan loaded up to go home. "We must take the long route to Middlegate, go around fifty miles to Fallon, then home. I have to finish my article for the magazine. It is due in a couple of days," explained Maggie.

Maggie called home, saying, "We'll be home by dark."

Sort of deja-vu, they returned to Luning, then up to Gabbs, staying on Hwy 361, and then drove on to Middlegate.

"The last time we were here, we had a waiter who was a murderer." They both laughed. "But they have the best burgers around," claimed Nan.

Maggie spoke into her tape recorder.

"Middlegate has a lot of history, surviving along 'The Loneliest Road in America,' Hwy 50, in Churchill County. It was originally named in the 1800s by James Simpson. This Sagebrush Saloon and Highway 50 rest stop got its name because of the gate-like mountains surrounding the stop. The community consists of about seventeen permanent residents on a good day. The Middlegate Station has a gas station, bar and restaurant, motel, and RV park. It once was a pony express station. They would change their horses here to continue their route.

A piece of trivia, Stephen King stayed here and wrote 'Desperation.' But the best part is their food. Anyone traveling this route needs to stop in and eat. So make this trip and go back in history.

They have a Doubledecker Burger to die for, which is one and third pounds of Angus beef on a sourdough bun, which I am going to have. I might even have a beer," laughed Maggie as she turned the recorder off.

"I think I will join you," laughed Nan. "One good thing here is not much snow. Guess there is something about being in the middle of the desert." And they both laughed as Maggie parked.

Maggie thought over the burger and beer, *glad this adventure worked out for everyone. Love those Wild Stitchers.*

They toasted each other. "Until our next adventure."

Made in the USA
Las Vegas, NV
10 August 2023

75905843R00069